Arthur A. Levine
Pearl Moscowitz's Last Stand

pictures by Robert Roth

TAMBOURINE BOOKS 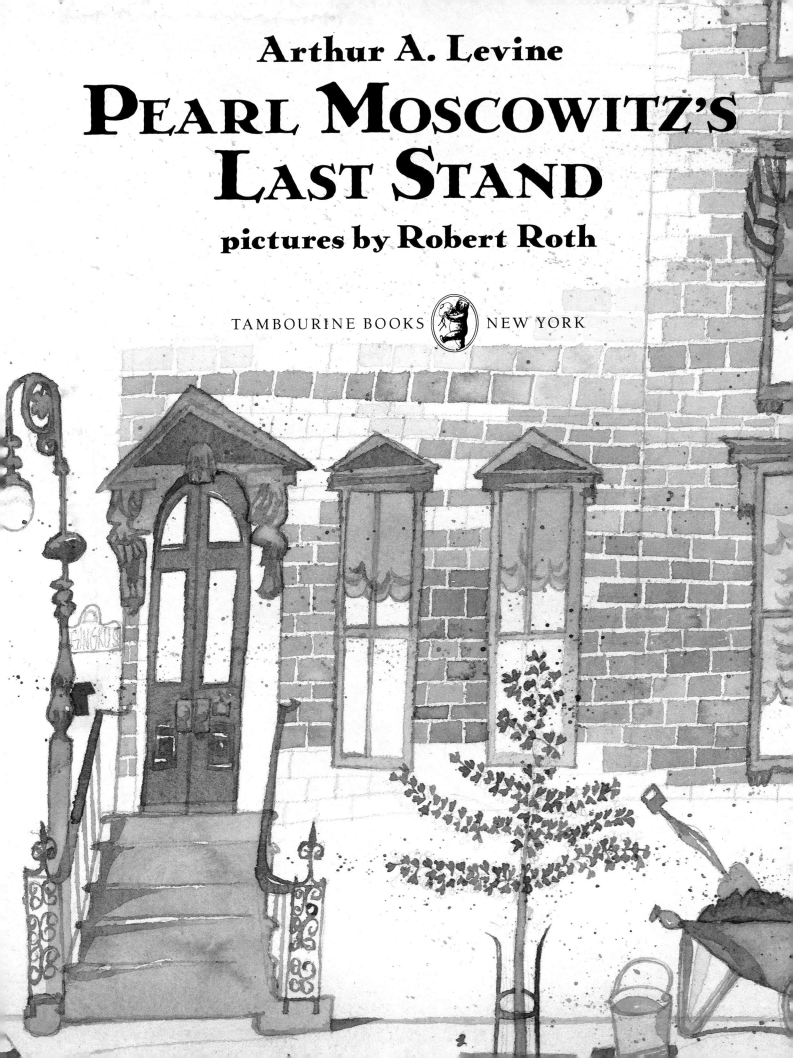 NEW YORK

For my mother, Eileen Levine—
tough as nails, sweet as tzimmes A.A.L.

To Mom and Dad R.R.

Library of Congress Cataloging in Publication Data

Levine, Arthur, 1962–   Pearl Moscowitz's last stand/by Arthur A. Levine;
pictures by Robert Roth—1st ed. p.   cm.
Summary: Pearl Moscowitz takes a stand when the city government
tries to chop down the last gingko tree on her street.
[1. Trees—Fiction.   2. City and town life—Fiction.]
I. Roth, Robert, ill.   II. Title.
PZ7.L57824Pe 1993 [E]—dc20 91-10652 CIP AC
ISBN 0-688-10753-2 (trade) — ISBN 0-688-10754-0 (lib.)
10 9 8 7 6 5 4 3 2 1
First edition

Pearl Moscowitz had seen a lot of change on Gingko Street.

In fact, she could remember when it was a plain street called Smith, after the man who paid for the signs. Mr. Smith.

But soon after the Brawarskys and Plotniks and Krakoffs started arriving from Russia there was a big change. Bella Moscowitz, Pearl's mother, gave a petition to the mayor asking for trees to be planted on the block. Flowering trees.

Who could argue with Bella?

He renamed the street for good measure.

So Pearl and her sisters Selma, Velma, and Wilma grew tall and blossomed next to nature's own. One fall the prettiest gingko tree of all was struck down by lightning and the sisters rushed out, crying, to gather the orphaned leaves. But the other gingkos thrived and one summer day Velma got married under the green canopy of Stuey Feinberg's tree.

Time passed and the names on the mailboxes changed to old presidents like Washington, Lincoln, and Jefferson. When Pearl sat out in the shade of the trees with her neighbors she began to serve mint tea and lemonade, "southern style." Her friends called her Puhhl. And Shugah.

And Pearl only minded a little when workers cleared away Minnie Hamilton's tree to make way for a bus stop. That made it easier for her sisters to visit.

So more time went by and families named Piña, Orantes, and Diego moved in. They taught Pearl to dance to a Latin beat. And they let her take a swing at the piñata for little Roy Diego's birthday party.

But one day a new mayor made a proclamation. "No more slums," he said. "Out with the old and in with the new." Bulldozers knocked down old town houses and took many of the trees with them. Pearl watched from her window and wished her mother were still alive. Bella would have stopped them.

DANGER WORK ZONE

By the time the Chens and the Kees became Pearl's neighbors, there was only one tree left. But it was a beauty—broad, strong, and deeply lined, not unlike Pearl herself. All the grandmas would gather under it to play cards and have picnics. Matzoh balls and steamed dumplings. Challah and jalapeños.

Then one day it happened. Pearl was sitting under the tree reading to Su-lin and Valerie from next door when a truck drove up. A tall, thin man with thin lips and a thin tie got out.

"Sorry folks, but you'll have to move," he said in a thin voice. "I have orders from the electric company to cut this tree down. New wiring. Regulations." Then he started laying out his tools.

Now as I said, Pearl had seen a lot of change on Gingko Street, but she was not about to sit idly by while they cut down the last gingko. She stood up.

"Excuse me," she said. "You look like a nice boy. Are you eating enough?"

The man looked up. "Well . . . I did skip lunch," he said.

"How about a nosh then. Girls?" said Pearl.

"Knishes!" shouted Su-lin.

"And bagels!" shouted Valerie.

"With plenty of cream cheese and lox," said Pearl. And she meant it. Out came plates, trays. Before he knew it, the man had tuna and kasha, some scrambled eggs, fresh fruit, a cheese plate, and Pearl's noodle pudding—so good and full of cinnamon it could stop you in your tracks. Cold.

The electrician was so stuffed he could barely move, let alone chop down a tree.

But the next day he was back. Pearl, Mrs. Char, Mrs. Washington, and Mrs. Guerrera were playing canasta under the tree. "OK, ladies, no snacks today. I mean business," said the man.

Pearl smiled. "Such a handsome boy," she whispered loudly to Mrs. Char. "And absolutely identical to my nephew Joseph." Pearl pulled out her wallet and opened it to the section for photos. "The resemblance is remarkable." The man couldn't help looking over Pearl's shoulder.

"Oh, honey, sit, we've got lots of pictures." The ladies snapped open their wallets into long plastic accordion folds. "And with each one, a story."

Let me tell you, no tree got chopped down *that* day. But would you believe this man came back for a third try the very next morning?

"This time no tricks," the man announced. Pearl looked up from fixing Ronnie Guerrera's bike. No one else was around.

"All right," said Pearl. "You leave me no choice." Very carefully she removed the long chain from Ronnie's bike.

With a bold but measured step she walked over to the tree and wrapped the chain around its trunk and hers. Then she had Ronnie lock his lock.

"Now go get your mother," Pearl told him. "It's time for canasta."

The ladies came and set up under the tree. Ronnie played Pearl's hand for her. Soon it was lunchtime and everyone set up a buffet.

Su-lin fed Pearl some cold sesame noodles and a Twinkie. "Are you all right?" the neighbors asked her.

"Fine," she said. "I'll be here as long as it takes."

People started leaning out their windows and coming down to see what was up. They brought music, baseballs, roller skates. It was the biggest party Gingko Street had ever seen.

Finally, just as the sun was setting, TV cameras showed up, and reporters interviewed Pearl. "I just want some justice," she told them. Of course, by then the mayor had arrived in a long black limousine.

"And it's justice you shall have!" proclaimed the mayor. He called off the cutting-down of the tree, and Pearl even made him promise to plant new gingkos up and down the block.

The neighbors cheered and set off fireworks long into the night. Pearl took the electrician and the mayor into her kitchen and gave them each a huge, warm slice of noodle pudding. The mayor had seconds.

Go look, I think he renamed the street.